# This book belongs to:

_____

A catalogue record for this book is available from the British Library

Published by Ladybird Books Ltd
80 Strand London WC2R 0RL
A Penguin Company

4 6 8 10 9 7 5 3
© LADYBIRD BOOKS LTD MMVI
LADYBIRD and the device of a Ladybird are trademarks of Ladybird Books Ltd

ISBN-13: 978-1-84646-072-2
ISBN-10: 1-84646-072-7

Printed in Italy

# The Magic Porridge Pot

illustrated by David Pace

The little girl

The old woman

4

The mother

The magic porridge pot

5

Once upon a time a little girl met an old woman.

The old woman gave her a magic porridge pot.

"Cook, little pot, cook," said the old woman.

And the little pot cooked some porridge.

9

"Stop, little pot, stop," said the old woman.

And the little pot stopped cooking.

The little girl took
the magic porridge
pot to her mother.

13

"Cook, little pot, cook," said the little girl's mother.

And the little pot cooked some porridge.

Soon the kitchen was full of porridge.

And still the magic porridge pot went on cooking.

Soon the house was full of porridge.

And still the magic porridge pot went on cooking.

19

Soon the street was full of porridge.

And still the magic porridge pot went on cooking.